Dragon Eggs Book 6

Dragon's First Valentine

Emily Martha Sorensen

Also by Emily Martha Sorensen

Wicked Witches of Restva:
Black Magic Academy

Fairy Senses:
Fairy Eyeglasses
Fairy Compass
Fairy Earmuffs
Fairy Barometer
Fairy Pox
Fairy Slippers
Fairy Lunchbox
Fairy Icepack
Fairy Stopwatch
Fairy Toothbrush
Fairy Perfume

Dragon Eggs:
Dragon's Egg
Dragon's Hope
Dragon's First Christmas
Dragon's Fire
Dragon's Song

Comics:
A Magical Roommate
To Prevent World Peace

Picture Books:
Tabby, Tabby, Burning Bright

The End in the Beginning:
The Keeper and the Rulership
The Fires of the Rulership
The Magic or the Rulership

Trilogy of a Teenage Werevulture:
Trials of a Teenage Werevulture
Trifles of a Teenage Werevulture
Weredodo Sleuth

The Numbers Just Keep
Getting Bigger:
Twenty-Four Potential
Children of Prophecy

Not Quite a Harem:
Not Quite a Curse

Magical Mayhem:
To Prevent World Peace
To Prevent Chic Costumes
To Prevent Clear Paths
To Prevent Smart Choices
To Prevent Warm Welcomes
To Prevent Cute Mascots
To Prevent First Place (prologue)
To Prevent Fresh Starts

Short Story Collections:
Worlds of Wonder
Magic and Mischief

To Ben,
the best husband ever.

Thank you for being my
always Valentine!

CHAPTER 1
Vexed

Rose woke up to the unmistakable sound of someone trying to be quiet.

"No no no no. No no no no. No no no no. No no no no —"

There was an earsplitting shriek.

Rose flung the blankets off her legs and stormed to the door of their bedroom, feeling rather vexed. She had asked to be permitted to sleep in this morning, seeing as it was Saturday and Henry's first class did not begin until eleven o'clock, but it seemed that was not to be. Why had Henry permitted the baby to get so close to the door where she was sleeping?

"Your mother's asleep," Henry's voice whispered in a frantic undertone from the other side of the door. "We can't disturb her. Just —"

Rose flung the door open.

Henry froze from a crouched position in the hallway.

Looking past him, Rose saw that there were flower petals scattered all down the length, and Virgil was currently rolling around in them. The baby dragon tried to shake a red flower petal off his vicious back claw, somersaulted into a sprawl, looked back, found it still stuck there, and let out another furious scream.

"I see he's managed to make a mess," Rose said dryly. "Where did he even find those?"

"He was supposed to be helping," Henry said sheepishly. He leapt to his feet and spread his arms. "Happy birthday!"

Rose blinked and looked down more closely. She supposed she could see how, if there had not been a baby dragon frolicking in them, those flower petals might have seemed romantic rather than looking like a florist's trash had been knocked over.

A better birthday present would have been an extra hour of sleep, Rose thought, exasperated.

But she knew her husband was not as practically-minded as she was. It was just like him to want to make a silly gesture like this. And she could appreciate the thought behind it.

"Thank you," Rose said. "What a nice present."

"Oh, that's not all," Henry said, bursting with pride. "Come into the living room!"

With some misgivings, Rose picked up Virgil and followed her husband down the hallway. The little dragon wiggled and complained and commented telepathically about the red thing stuck on his back claw that wouldn't come off and it was stuck and he wanted to breathe fire at it but he didn't have fire in his tummy right now!

Rose paid him no heed. She was too frozen with horror at the sight before her.

Twenty vases.

Twelve flowers in each vase.

There were twenty *dozen* roses.

"How —?" Rose asked, her voice rising in a panicked squeak.

"I bought them," Henry said proudly. "See, your name's Rose, and it's your twentieth birthday —"

"It's two days to Valentine's Day!" Rose cried, hyperventilating. "Why would you not ask me before making such an extravagant purchase? Why would you purchase twenty dozen flowers at the most expensive time of the year? Why would you purchase twenty dozen flowers *anyway?!*"

Henry looked hurt. "It was a present —"

Chapter 1: Vexed

"This is not a present!" Rose exclaimed. "This is *bankruptcy!*"

Henry's face turned red. "I was just trying to be thoughtful!"

"Then *think* about things! Just because I'm taking care of the budget now doesn't mean it's not a good idea to look at the book once in awhile!"

"We're not *that* poor!" Henry exclaimed.

"How would you know?! You're terrible at sums!"

She knew at once that it was the wrong thing to say.

Her husband spun around, flung open the door to the apartment, and stalked out, slamming the door behind him.

Rose flopped onto the couch, trying to put her head in her hands. Since their dragon son was still in her arms, he made a spiny, wiggly barrier.

Why was Virgil's mother upset? Virgil's father thought the red things were pretty.

"They are pretty," Rose mumbled, moving the baby dragon onto her lap and successfully depositing her forehead into her hands this time. "They're also completely impractical. Why couldn't he have bought me a new saucepan or something?"

Virgil's father liked pretty things. Virgil's father never thought they had enough pretty things. Virgil's father had been excited about buying Virgil's mother the present. Virgil had gone with his father. It had been fun! He'd only broken one of the vases while they were there.

Rose sighed heavily.

She'd handled it wrong. She knew she had. It really had been a thoughtful gesture. She had no doubt that if she did something this ridiculous to celebrate his birthday, he would be thrilled.

But she couldn't do something this ridiculous. That was the whole point. Their monetary situation was tight enough as it was. Keeping Virgil fed was a constant struggle, given that their dragon son ate more and more every month and still adamantly refused to try anything less expensive than chicken, such as pork or even the cheapest cuts of beef. He was even starting to object to having eggs mixed in with his chicken, since he preferred the meat.

Rose would *not* allow their picky eater to win that battle, thanks very much.

It would be very helpful if their son were capable of eating plants, but *Deinonychus antirrhopus* was a carnivorous species, so there was nothing that could be done about that. It was hard not to resent her son's diet when she and Henry had not bought any meat for themselves in over a month, however.

And now this! Why had Henry thought this present was a good idea? Why?

Virgil vigorously kicked his back foot, and Rose narrowly escaped having the wicked hooked claw slice at her elbow.

He wanted the thing off now! Off! Off! Off! Off!

Rose carefully removed the rose petal from around her son's hooked claw, a rather difficult feat to accomplish without being speared, given that he kept on kicking with it.

The front door opened, and Henry reappeared.

"Henry!" Rose said with relief. "I apologize that I —"

"No," Henry said in a low voice. He squared his shoulders and looked up. "I was thinking about what *I* wanted, not what *you* wanted. I . . . should've thought more. I'll see if the florist will let me return them."

Rose swallowed. The thought filled her with relief, and that made her feel guilty. Henry had probably been really excited about this gift. "It *was* a thoughtful present —"

"No, it was a stupid present, just as you said," he shot back flatly. "I should've bought you a book about dragon bones, or something."

That would have been a lovely gift, yes. Rose bit her lip, wishing she could think of an honest way to contradict him.

Henry gathered up the vases of flowers, two at a time, and took them outside. It took him ten trips. Then he got the wooden wagon out of the hall closet and took it outside, as well.

Rose got up from the couch and followed him out of the apartment. He was now walking up and down the stairs carrying the wagon, then a few vases, then the wagon, then a few more vases from one landing to another.

Chapter 1: Vexed

He must have done this all the way up, she realized. *And carrying Virgil, as well. How much effort did he put forth?*

"Would you like help?" Rose asked.

"No, thank you."

"But I'd be happy to —"

"It's your birthday," Henry said stubbornly. "It's my mess. I'll fix it."

Rose headed back into the apartment, where she found Virgil had already crawled into his bucket, and was now happily rolling around the room and whamming into the wall over and over again.

Slam! Slam! Slam! Slam!

She sighed heavily.

"Happy birthday," she murmured.

CHAPTER 2
Voracious

Fixing breakfast, Rose went to dispose of the eggshells and discovered a dozen rose stems in the trash. She pulled them out and looked at them, then walked over to the hallway, where — sure enough — she counted enough rose petals to have come from twelve beheaded roses.

Rose sighed heavily. *So he can't return all of them. He had already deconstructed a dozen he'd bought for that purpose.*

Still — a single dozen was not going to ruin them. And there was nothing that could be done.

Behind her, Virgil let out a gale of amusement at having discovered a new game of pick-up-a-rose-petal-with-his-teeth-and-blow-it-out-in-the-air.

By the time Henry got back home, Rose had prepared a breakfast of pancakes for both of them, and Virgil was halfway through his raw eggs mixed with water and chicken.

Henry came through the door with the wagon under his arm. There were no roses or vases present, which was a relief.

"Good morning," Rose said. She did not mention the rose petals, which she had gathered into a bowl on the top of their dresser. She would, perhaps, make potpourri from them later.

"Good morning," Henry said, depositing the wagon into the hall closet. He did not mention the rose petals, either.

Chapter 2: Voracious

Rose was dying to ask if the florist had taken the flowers back and returned their money, but she didn't see how she could do so without seeming overly eager for the disposal of her birthday present, so she kept her silence.

Henry sat down at the table and stared wistfully at the stack of pancakes on a plate by the stove, his eyes communicating that he didn't know whether he was allowed to eat them.

Taking the hint, Rose smiled and took the plate over to him. Looking relieved, he eagerly helped himself.

"I've already had mine," Rose said. "I hope you don't mind."

"Why would I mind?" Henry asked between bites. "It's your birthday. You can do whatever you want."

She was still dying to ask about the florist and whether they had gotten all of their money back, but she didn't want to spoil the congenial atmosphere. They must have gotten it all back, mustn't they? Surely they had.

She didn't want to make demands of Henry when his ego was no doubt fragile. Doing that would be —

Virgil had eaten his food! Virgil wanted more food! More food, more food, more food!

Rose glanced over to see that Virgil had made his way across the room in a flash, and was now trying to claw his way up to Henry's lap.

The attempt was, of course, piercing tiny holes all over the pant legs. But the one bright side of this was that no one would be able to distinguish them from the many other tiny holes Virgil had left before. There was a reason Henry did not wear his nicest clothing around the house. Neither did Rose.

"Of course you do, you exasperating boy," Henry said, picking the little dragon up. "One might say that's the source of all our problems."

Virgil nuzzled his father with his snout. He liked food. Could he have food again? He wanted chicken all by itself this time. He liked chicken the best. He wanted chicken, chicken, chicken, all by itself.

"No," Rose said. "Don't pretend to be voracious."

Virgil pointedly ignored this, emanating pitiful memories of hunger as he curled his tail around his father's wrist. Could he have chicken, chicken, chicken? He was still hungry. He was still very hungry. His father didn't want him to starve, did he?

"Well . . ." Henry hesitated. "I mean, if he's still hungry . . ."

"Hey, Virgil," Rose said, picking up a slice of pancake from off his father's plate. "You can have chicken if you eat this first."

The little dragon exploded off his father's lap and raced into the other room.

No yucky! No yucky yucky! Virgil wouldn't eat yucky food! Virgil wasn't hungry!

"Are you sure he *isn't* hungry, though?" Henry asked.

"If he were hungry, he would have finished off the food in his bowl," Rose said dryly, picking up their son's food bowl and displaying the interior. The boy had polished off every scrap of chicken, but there were still gooey patches of egg. "He also would have been a lot less cute and manipulative."

Henry laughed. "Okay. He got me."

"Honestly," Rose said with exasperation, covering the food bowl with its lid and placing it in the icebox, so that she could get the boy to finish the eggs later. "We've got to find something less expensive that he's willing to eat."

"You could ask the Lawrences what they're feeding Ophelia," Henry said. "She's clearly healthy, and I suspect they have less money than we do."

Rose hesitated. While Alice and Willie seemed like very nice people, she hadn't really made their acquaintance well enough to show up at their home unannounced. Not to mention that . . . well . . . she was white and they were colored, and she wasn't sure if there were rules against her doing such a thing.

"We could call Mr. Teedle and ask if they have a phone," Henry said.

"Yes! A phone!" Rose said with relief. Surely there could be no rules of propriety against that. And then, if they invited her to come over to visit, she would graciously accept and know that it was acceptable by any relevant social rules.

Chapter 2: Voracious

A phone. Of course, a phone. Why had she not thought of that herself?

"You're brilliant," she informed Henry.

He snorted. "I think I've shown today that I am certainly not."

"Making mistakes doesn't make one not capable of brilliance," Rose said. She hesitated. "Did the florist take the flowers back?"

"Yes. Although he said he wouldn't have if it were Easter." Henry gave her a tentative and sheepish smile. "Apparently that's their largest holiday of the year."

"Then let us not buy flowers around Easter," Rose said.

"So, what *do* you want to do to celebrate Valentine's Day?" Henry blurted out. "I was thinking the flowers would be part of that celebration, too. That's why it seemed so perfect. I want us to do something special. It's our first one together, after all."

Rose blinked. "I . . . I don't know."

Why did it matter so much to him? It really wasn't that important a holiday, unlike Christmas or Easter.

"I've never known my parents to celebrate Valentine's Day," she went on. "A wedding anniversary is more important."

"That's just it!" Henry cried. "Our wedding anniversary is on the same day as Virgil's birthday! If we want to have a day that's just about us, it has to be Valentine's Day!"

Ah. He did have a point, she supposed.

"We could always choose a different day to celebrate," she pointed out. "Like the day we met, for instance, or the day you proposed to me —"

"Those were both the same day, and it was also the day we met Virgil!" Henry said. "I don't want our relationship to be all about Virgil!"

Small chance of that, given that Virgil is the reason we got married in the first place, Rose thought tartly, but that didn't seem to be the answer Henry wanted right now.

"I will think about it," Rose said carefully. "Perhaps we can ask my parents to watch Virgil, and we can go out to the theater or something."

"And spend more money?" Henry asked gloomily.

"For a special occasion, and an expense we both agree to, yes."

Henry didn't look very excited by the prospect.

"Or my parents could watch Virgil for the night."

"How would that be any different from normal?" Henry complained. "It's not like we don't have time together when he's asleep. It's just . . . the flowers were what was going to make it special!"

Rose was starting to feel rather exasperated. *Apparently I should buy him flowers for his birthday.*

She made a mental note to write that down. It might actually be a good idea.

Not twenty dozen, though, for crying out loud.

"Well, what do you want to do?" Rose asked in a sensible tone. "We can do whatever you like."

"I want to do what *you* want to do," Henry said stubbornly.

So now she was expected to come up with something that she personally wanted to do that Henry would consider romantic enough for an outing on Valentine's Day? Something other than ignoring the event altogether?

Rose wanted to throw up her hands at the impossible assignment. Why couldn't he settle for her merely being willing to humor him and tolerate whatever he wanted to do?

Virgil snuck back into the kitchen, his eyes gleaming.

He spotted the source of his food. If he could butcher it, it would reveal its yummy innards to him.

"It's not prey," Rose said dryly. "You can't kill it."

Virgil could try!

The tiny dragon launched himself at the icebox, trying desperately to slaughter it.

Henry doubled over laughing.

CHAPTER 3
Variety

One would think one's birthday would be a special time, different from any ordinary day. But once Henry had left for his eleven o'clock class, Rose found herself entrenched back in her usual Tuesday, Thursday, and Saturday routine.

Washing the breakfast dishes. Changing Virgil's diaper. Studying her textbook. Changing Virgil's diaper. Ignoring his not-so-subtle hints that he wanted chicken without egg as a snack before lunch. Changing Virgil's diaper.

Making sure he breathed fire in the bathroom, rather than all over the couch. Changing Virgil's diaper. Stopping him from shredding a stinky diaper. Changing Virgil's diaper. Washing the stack of diapers from the day so far so that they would have more clean ones. Changing Virgil's diaper.

"Maybe we should start to potty-train you," Rose said dryly.

Virgil looked up from having the sides of the cloth pinned across his hindquarters. He didn't understand what that meant.

"It means teaching you to use the toilet, not a diaper."

Virgil didn't understand what that meant.

Rose pictured the bathroom and imagined Virgil making use of the facilities in a way she desperately wished the boy would learn soon.

Virgil let out a shrill squeal and raced into the bedroom and scrambled under the bed. No! No, no! He wouldn't do that! He would hide way out of his mother's reach!

He didn't seem to notice that his tail was sticking out by over a foot.

"For crying out loud," Rose said in exasperation, reaching under there and tugging him out, gently, by a back foot. She was tempted to use the tail, but she wasn't sure if that was more fragile than the rest of him. The back foot, though, she knew from experience, was strong enough to be fine to drag him out with. "You're going to have to learn eventually."

No! The big white hole was scary! It made noises and things fell into it and never came out again!

"Yes," Rose said. "That is the point."

No! Nooooooo! Virgil wouldn't do it! Virgil wouldn't ever, ever do it!

"You most certainly will," Rose said waspishly.

Virgil was being dragged out from under the bed! Virgil hated it! Virgil wanted to hide! Virgil was going to kick his mother with his hooked claws!

Rose dodged the assault, just barely. The vicious attack only made her more peeved.

"If you do that again, you're going to be in time-out in the bathtub for the rest of the day," she snapped. "It is not fine to attack me. That could hurt me badly. My skin is more vulnerable than your scales. Do you understand?"

Virgil didn't understand and Virgil wasn't happy and Virgil's mother was mean and Virgil's father was nice and Virgil didn't want to go in the white box! The white box was boring!

"And yet, I remain unmoved," Rose said coldly.

Virgil let out an earsplitting shriek, and she covered her ears to protect her hearing. Above them, she thought she heard a neighbor pounding loudly on their ceiling. There was an odd tenor to the scream this time, as if a phone were simultaneously ringing. Had Virgil developed a new pitch? If so, that was going to be quite annoying . . .

Wait — the phone *was* ringing!

Rose leapt up, hands still over her ears, and dashed to the kitchen. Removing her hands from her ears, she answered the phone before the ringing stopped.

"Hello? Wainscott residence?" she said, panting.

"Hello, Miss Palmer," the familiar voice of an old friend said warmly. "Er — Mrs. Wainscott. How are you this morning?"

"About as well as could be expected," Rose said politely, which was not precisely a lie. Virgil was all too often as poorly behaved as this. "Henry and I were just talking about calling you, Mr. Teedle. How is your day?"

"Oh, quite well, quite well," he said. "We have a visitor at the museum who is asking about you today."

"Really?" Rose asked, her eyebrows rising. She could not imagine who that might be. She was hardly famous. While she was going to become a paleontologist once she completed her education, she was currently only beginning her bachelor's degree, with a major in geology. It would be many years before she would be trusted to handle real fossils in a laboratory. Given that, who in the field knew her name?

"Yes. His name is Mr. Miller. He's from Chicago. He has a daughter who hatched out of the Field Museum of Natural History. He thought it would be nice for them to meet you and your son. He would have liked to have met your husband too, but I know that he's busy at school on this day of the week."

Rose's heart fell like a stone. Of course it was about Virgil. Everything was about Virgil. Nobody ever found her interesting all by herself.

"How nice," she said, hoping she successfully sounded as if she meant it. "Would he like to arrange a meeting with the other baby dragons, as well?"

"Oh, he's already met Ophelia," Mr. Teedle said. "He and his daughter went to see her vaudeville performance last night. That was why they came into town. And they've already visited Violet at the zoo. I'm afraid the Baileys weren't at home when they called, or so their maid informed them."

So that makes Virgil their fourth choice?

Rose tried not to be offended. It was true that two of the four baby dragons in New York were now minor celebrities, while the Baileys were public figures due to their wealth, so it made sense that she and Henry would be the least interesting choice to a visitor from out of town.

Still. Virgil had been the first dragon to hatch in their city. That should mean something.

". . . be able to arrange a meeting today, before he goes back home tomorrow?" Mr. Teedle was saying.

Rose drew in a deep breath. She would be a fool to say no. She was legitimately interested in meeting every dragon in the country. Besides, it would be something to make her birthday a unique day, even if the situation was all about Virgil.

"Yes, I would be happy to bring Virgil to meet with them," Rose said. "We have several hours available right now. When and where should we meet?"

There was a murmur of voices. It seemed the man was right there, and Mr. Teedle was conferring with him.

"How about the northwest corner of Central Park?" Mr. Teedle said at last. "It is reasonably centrally located between where you live and where he is now, so it will take you both only about half an hour to walk there. The children will have space to run around and play in the grass, too."

And hopefully not burn down the trees, Rose thought, but she didn't raise the objection. It would probably be fine.

"I will get Virgil ready and depart in just a few minutes," Rose said. "I look forward to meeting Mr. Miller and his daughter. How old is she, anyway?" she added curiously.

"Almost three months," Mr. Teedle said.

So she would be at about the size Virgil had been during Christmas, and not a fragile newborn who could not even roll over successfully. That was good.

"I'll see him there in half an hour, then," Rose said. "I'm sure we'll have no trouble finding each other, seeing as there will be no other infant dragons around. Oh, what is his daughter's —"

A terrible odor reached her nose. She looked through the doorway to see Virgil rolling across the floor of the living room, diaper sagging, one side of it shredded by a vicious back claw, trailing an officious disaster on the carpet behind him.

As she stared in horror, he rolled backwards right over the catastrophe.

"Fifteen minutes! We'll leave in fifteen minutes!" Rose cried in horror and slammed the phone into its cradle. Then she bolted to the living room to seize her son before he could make the nightmare any worse.

Holding the boy out at an arm's length, she raced for the bathroom, where she commenced to give a screaming dragon a bath that he did not want for a reason she enjoyed even less. Naturally, the neighbor above added to the stress by pounding on his floor, their ceiling, again.

The more she thought about it, the more glad she was that they would be departing the apartment soon. At least it would give this dreadful-so-far day some variety.

CHAPTER 4
Verdant

It took twice as long as she expected before they left, due to Virgil's mess being even more disgusting and laborious to clean up than she had realized.

Still, within half an hour, she had him clean and the carpet recovered, save for some stains she could not seem to fix. Once they left, she rushed down the sidewalk on the way to Central Park as swiftly as possible, humiliatingly aware that she was already late.

The wooden wagon she was pulling behind her attracted far more attention than the pram had, due to Virgil being far more visible and far more difficult to cover with a blanket. Virgil seemed amused by all the extra attention, making lots of comments to all the people who passed and stared at him with their mouths agape.

Yes, I realize Virgil is fascinating, Rose thought grumpily, refusing to stop to converse with several passersby who called out questions to her. *But I am not subject to your beck and call just because you are curious about him.*

Reaching the northwest corner of Central Park, she soon discovered there was a crowd gathered, gasping and chattering excitedly over something.

Chapter 4: Verdant

With a sinking heart, Rose realized what was going on. It was the same phenomenon that she had just experienced while walking here. Of course anyone passing by would stop to watch an adorable dragon frolicking on the grass. By meeting out in public, they had made plans to provide a public circus.

Unfortunately, there was very little they could do about it at this point. To ask people to leave would be rude. Besides, she doubted it would do any good. More curious onlookers would only gather in their place.

Rose picked up Virgil, likewise collected the bulky wagon, tucked each determinedly under one arm, and shoved her way through the crowd to reach the center of it.

Sure enough, in a grassy spot beside the sidewalk, a man sat beside an unfamiliar dragon who was rolling around on the grass. Surprisingly, the other dragon was almost the same color as Virgil, just a little brighter — a verdant green.

The unfamiliar emerald-colored dragon was eyeing a stem of dead grass, drifting back and forth in a breeze, and then she suddenly sprang forward to catch it, capturing the dead grass prey in her mouth.

She spat it out a second later, and she probably made some sort of telepathic comment, because the people near the front of the crowd laughed.

"Hello!" the man standing behind her cried, spying Rose with her son tucked under one arm and the bulky wagon under the other. He stood up and strode over to her, holding out his hand to shake. "I'm James Miller. And you're Rose Wainscott, I believe?"

Rose set down the bulky wagon, shifted Virgil to her left arm, and shook his hand with her right. "Yes, I am. I'm pleased to meet you, Mr. Miller. This is Virgil."

"He's almost the same color as Cucumber!" Mr. Miller said in delight. He reached out and patted Virgil across the back. "We don't have any other green dragons in Chicago. Just red and purple."

"How many do you have now?" Rose asked.

"Three. Out of the eight eggs in the Field Museum. The third one just barely hatched. Our daughter was the second."

"And you said her name, was, uh . . .?" Rose prompted, unable to believe she had heard him correctly before.

"Cucumber," he said. "Cukie for short. Because she's green, you know."

Rose wanted to cover her face with her hands. What kind of name was that for a child? Why would anyone name their daughter such a thing?

"The other two back home are named Rosie and Plum," the man added.

"Rosie is red and Plum is purple," Rose said flatly.

Mr. Miller looked surprised. "How did you know?"

Rose tried hard not to give him an incredulous look.

So it was becoming a tradition in Chicago to name dragons after their scale color, was it? She supposed it was better than naming them things like Claws or Spiny, but only just. Hopefully the next dragon to hatch there would have parents with the good sense to break out of that ridiculous tradition.

"Well, would you like to play with . . . Cucumber, Virgil?" she asked, setting her son down on the grass relatively near the other dragon. "She's just a little younger than Violet's age, so you can play the same games you play with Violet."

Virgil completely ignored this invitation. He turned his back on the other dragon and started digging at the dead grass, which was for once not covered with frost or snow, it being an unseasonably warm day. At least the insects had not started to come out of hiding yet.

Virgil raised his head in interest. What were those little things Virgil's mother was thinking about? Were they edible?

Rose was distracted for a moment by the intriguing idea that Virgil's question posed. *Could* he eat insects? Would those do to supplement his diet?

But then she remembered their early experiment with feeding him a cricket. It had not agreed with him, and she had no desire to ever again have to clean up dragon vomit.

"Don't eat them," Rose said quickly. "Virgil, come over here and play with Cucumber. She's a new dragon you've never met before who's close to your age."

Virgil turned a deaf ear to this invitation.

Meanwhile, Mr. Miller was trying unsuccessfully to cajole his uncooperative daughter to do the same thing.

"Virgil, Cukie," he was saying. "Go play with Virgil. He's the little dragon over there. Come on, you loved playing with Violet and Ophy. What's the problem here?"

Cucumber continued to ignore him.

Exasperated, Rose picked up Virgil and hauled him over, depositing him right next to Cucumber.

That got a reaction.

Icky! Icky, icky, icky! Cucumber couldn't play with him! He was *green!*

Yucky! Yucky, yucky, yucky! That girl was green! Green, green, green, green!

"What in the world?" Rose said in bafflement. "*You're* green!"

Yes! Virgil was green! GREEN! GREEN!

As if Virgil's panic was catching, Cucumber let out a loud shriek, causing the members of the crowd to gasp, hold their hands over their ears, and in some cases actually run away.

If only, Rose reflected, they could induce the rest of the crowd to leave without resorting to such a thing.

Cucumber's panic was now at an even higher pitch than Virgil's.

GREEN! GREEN! He was a boy, and he was GREEN!

Virgil backed away, emanating the same horror. GREEN! She was a girl, and she was GREEN!

"What in the world is wrong with you two?" Rose exclaimed. "You're both green!"

GREEN! GREEN GREEN GREEN!

Both the dragons were scrambling away from each other and flashing memories of the same color in absolute horror.

"What . . .?" Mr. Miller said in bewilderment.

Green GIRL!

Green BOY!

GREEN GREEN GREEN!

Rose's mouth fell open. She had an odd suspicion . . .

"Virgil," she said rapidly, "if Cucumber were a boy, would that be a problem?"

Green boys weren't yucky! Only green girls were!

Wrong! Green girls weren't icky! Only green boys were!

"*What?*" Mr. Miller exclaimed.

"Inbreeding!" Rose cried, clapping her hands.

What delightful serendipity this had turned out to be, having her son meet a female dragon who was the same color as him. She would never have seen this in action without such a bizarre happening. She would never have even guessed that such a behavior existed!

"Inbreeding!" Rose cried, clapping her hands again. "It's an instinct to discourage inbreeding! I've wondered why there were so many different colors of the same species living within a tiny geographic area! Now we have our answer!"

"*What?!*" Mr. Miller looked completely baffled.

Rose grinned, feeling a thrill of discovery. She had figured something out that perhaps no one else had had the opportunity to infer yet. This was a birthday present indeed!

CHAPTER 5
Victim

Green dragons separated from each other and scrambled across the grass. Once they were a comfortable distance of at least five feet away, the two infant dragons recommenced ignoring one another.

"What are you talking about?" the man asked.

"Oh." Rose blinked. "I assume you know that natural selection favors a diversity of traits within a species."

The man had a blank look.

"It's important to have varied genes within a population of a species so that it stays evolutionarily flexible."

This did not seem to enlighten the man.

"Humans have a taboo against inbreeding, which is the reason we don't usually marry siblings," Rose explained. "I should have realized dragons had an instinct like this. In one of Violet's mother's memories, she was thinking that the male she was chasing after was purple and thus a different color from her own blue, showing that they weren't closely related. So *Deinonychus* dragons must have an instinct to avoid potential mates who are the same color!"

"But they're *babies!*" Mr. Miller exclaimed.

"What has that to do with it?"

"Babies don't have potential mates!"

This man did not seem to understand how biology worked.

"Babies grow into adults eventually," Rose said. "If they have a deep-rooted instinct from infancy to not even befriend a member of the opposite gender with the same color, that would be effective to prevent any friendships forming that might develop into romantic attachments later."

"But they're *babies!*"

This man seemed to be a little dim.

"The instinct wouldn't cause problems with infants surviving, so there's no reason it shouldn't be present now."

"But it would!" Mr. Miller cried. "What about parents and children? They'd be closely related and often the same color!"

Rose pondered that. "I'd have to assume the instinct only applies to individuals close to one's own age," she said at last.

"What about brothers and sisters?" Mr. Miller shot back. "Children have to be able to get along with their siblings!"

"Really? Why?" Rose asked coolly. "There's no reason to assume that is an evolutionary necessity. Besides, look at them."

Virgil was now busily digging up dirt with his claws, while Cucumber was preparing to pounce on another clump of dead grass, to the great amusement of the crowd around them.

"They're ignoring one another. They only became aggressive about their aversion to each other when forced together. Dragon parents would know better than to do such a thing. Thus, the instinct would not cause any particular problems with the survival of one's family members."

Another idea occurred to her.

"In addition, remember that this instinct would mean virtually all dragon parents would be different colors from each other. Thus, the chances of their children being different colors from each other would be quite high. When you add to this the fact that they apparently would not feel discomfort in being near a member of the same gender and same color, this means the chances of potential conflict between siblings are probably no higher than one-in-four."

"That's still very high!"

Rose shrugged. "Not high enough to be a problem."

"One-in-four isn't high enough?!"

"Not really, evolutionarily speaking," Rose said. "Especially since the instinct doesn't even seem to incite them to violence. I imagine any disadvantages are outweighed by the advantages, which was why the instinct survived."

Rose stared at her son, fascinated, as the man murmured under his breath.

What could she do to test this hypothesis? She could pick up Virgil and bring him closer to Cucumber by increments, to see how close a range it took to set off their mutual alarm. Perhaps if they were forced to touch each other, it might actually result in violence — that would be another hypothesis worth testing. Really, this was quite a strange and captivating instinct, in so many ways the opposite of humanity.

Rose moved forward to pick up her son —

She stopped abruptly.

Her son.

Virgil was *her son.*

What kind of person thought it would be fascinating to test if they could get two infants to attack each other?

What kind of parent was she?

Rose backed away, clenching her fists. Her inadequacy as a parent was appalling. Did she lack even the most basic scraps of decency?

"Come on, Cucumber," Mr. Miller said, stooping to pick up his daughter. "You can get over this. You can make friends —"

GREEN! GREEN GREEN GREEN!

Rose sighed. The other parent present, it seemed, was just an idiot.

But really, this was a frustrating position to be in. She itched to study this hypothesis and find out if it was correct. At the very least, she wanted to sit down with a baby dragon and interview them exhaustively about every possible facet of *Deinonychus* society.

She couldn't do that with Virgil, because she had promised herself she would never look at him as a subject to scrutinize and study. And with good reason, apparently.

She couldn't do that with Violet, because the blue dragon who lived in the zoo had answered human questions about her society so often that her memories had become completely corrupted by imagination and interpretation.

She couldn't do that with Philomel, because she could not bring herself to want to spend one minute in the presence of his mother that she did not have to.

She couldn't do that with Ophelia, because . . . well, perhaps she *could* do that with Ophelia, but only if she overcame her overwhelming awkwardness at the thought of trying to make her parents' further acquaintance.

But *this* dragon . . . this dragon named Cucumber, such a terrible name . . .

Rose's eyes fell on the infant whose father was trying unsuccessfully to convince her to play with the green little boy she was studiously ignoring.

Cucumber did not live in New York City. She would not be one of Virgil's playmates. Rose did not have to be worried what this dragon's father would think of her, because she would most likely never see him again.

So she could be bold. What was the worst that he could say to her? No?

Rose drew in a deep breath. "Mr. Miller, would you allow me to interview Cucumber about her memories of dragon society? She might remember things that my son does not. If you want to, you could talk to Virgil about the same thing."

"Oh, I've already interviewed Cukie pretty thoroughly about her memories before she woke up back home," the man said matter-of-factly. "I've written it all down, too. I don't think there's much I don't know. But then again, *this* surprised me . . ."

He gestured at his daughter, who was desperately trying to wriggle out of his arms and away from Virgil, who was stepping on crumbling brown leaves and ignoring her.

Chapter 5: Victim

"So maybe you'll think to ask some questions I haven't, and learn some things I don't know. As long as you write everything down and give me a copy, that sounds good to me. The first time she remembers something new, it needs be recorded, of course."

Rose's voice failed her.

Of course.

He had said that as if it were obvious.

And now that she thought about it, it was.

Of course it was obvious that a dragon's uncorrupted memories of their original family should be preserved as early as possible. Of course it was an evident necessity to record every detail of *Deinonychus antirrhopus* society before the memories of that were influenced by living among humans.

Every clue was a piece of a fragile puzzle that would swiftly degrade. And yet, she had not recorded even one of Virgil's memories in writing. It had not even crossed her mind.

It was as if she had discovered a priceless treasure, a bone of some never-before-seen species, and then dug it up with a careless shovel, leaving the edges irreparably damaged.

This man was not an idiot, as she had supposed. *She* was the fool.

What Virgil had forgotten or altered by now could never be regained. Every memory of his time before humans had been affected by his life now and transmuted into a different state. She knew that. She had seen it happening.

The only way to capture her son's memories in a pure state was to write them down. The transmission of telepathic memory was no more than an oral tradition, fragile and easily mutated.

Virgil was the victim of her own foolishness. Of her ability to know and not *see.*

"Of course I will record whatever she says," Rose said, finding her voice at last. "And will you also do the same for me?"

Her son must not be a victim of her blindness any longer. Not now that her eyes were open to what she should have been doing in the first place.

CHAPTER 6
Vindicated

Before anything else, it was necessary that they escape from the swarming crowd and find a place to interview the children with a modicum more privacy. One obvious place that sprang to mind was the Research Library at the American Museum of Natural History, which was open to the public and yet not a place large quantities of crowds tended to gather in. In a way, it was even appropriate, since research about dragons was precisely what Rose wanted to do.

She picked up her son, who protested vigorously about having to leave his dirt, and placed him in the wagon.

"Are you sure they'll want small children there?" Mr. Miller asked when Rose voiced her plan for their relocation.

Rose paused. Fire-breathing infants would probably not be considered the ideal patrons of the Research Library, no.

"We can ask Mr. Teedle to lend us his office," she decided. "Or some other private room. I'm sure he would be happy to oblige."

"Oh, yes, he's a nice man," Mr. Miller said, nodding. "I asked him what to do when Cukie has nightmares, and he told me about what worked with his daughters."

"Does Cucumber have nocturnal terrors, too?" Rose asked with avid interest. "Violet, the blue dragon, does."

"All the dragons do, don't they?" Mr. Miller said, picking up his daughter, who thrashed, trying to escape back to the ground. "They all remember losing their original parents."

Rose was silent. Her son did not suffer from bad dreams. He was a pretty sound sleeper. It had not occurred to her that that was one way in which she and Henry were blessed. And Virgil, of course, because not suffering from panic on a regular basis like Violet did was certainly a privilege for him.

"Do Rosie and Plum suffer from nightmares, too?" she asked, as the two commenced walking down the sidewalk.

The crowd, more's the pity, surged after them. A few unwanted gawkers and bystanders took the hint and wandered away, but most continued to stroll after, giggling as Virgil tried to roll over backwards inside the wagon, a feat he had never accomplished even in less limited space, and then made commentary on how it would be easier if his tail didn't keep getting in the way.

The crowd seemed greatly amused by this, and there were many giggles at his persistence as he attempted to do it again.

"Rosie, yes," Mr. Miller said. "Plum, sometimes. Not so often. Plum has other issues Dr. McGrath has to help with. Poor kid; she thinks he might have something similar to diabetes. He's not a very healthy dragon."

Rose was startled. "Is Dr. McGrath . . . a woman?"

She'd heard of female doctors, but she had never actually met one.

Mr. Miller laughed. "I said the same thing when I met her! She told me she's one of the first . . . what . . . five female veterinarians in the country? Anyway, she specializes in small animals rather than horses, unlike most veterinarians, so she's pretty much the local expert on dragons these days."

Rose felt a stab of intense envy. Imagine living in the same city as a woman like that! What conversations she could have with such a remarkable person!

Cucumber suddenly hissed and stabbed her father in the arm with her claw.

"Ouch!" he shouted. "Cukie!"

Cucumber was bored! Cucumber wanted to get down and play some more! Cucumber wanted to get down, or she would claw her father again!

Mr. Miller quickly moved to dump her in the wagon.

"No! Wait —" Rose cried.

GREEN! GREEN GREEN GREEN GREEN!

Two infant dragons scrambled for the edges of the wagon, trying desperately to climb out. Cucumber bashed her head against the sides in fruitless attempts. Virgil actually succeeded, tumbling headlong over the side. Rose barely caught him in time to protect his cranium from crashing into the pavement.

"Virgil!" Rose said in exasperation. Her young son figuring out how to escape his wagon at a moment's notice was not a milestone she had eagerly anticipated.

Virgil looked up at her with pitiful eyes. But *green*.

Rose sighed and put a hand to her forehead.

"Cukie, let's get out of their wagon now," Mr. Miller cajoled, reaching for his daughter.

The female dragon swiped at her father's fingers.

No! She wanted to stay here! This was an interesting place!

"I see she is in the mood to be disobliging," Rose said dryly.

"I'm sorry," Mr. Miller sighed, adjusting his hat wearily. It was a rather worn fedora that had small holes and loose threads all over. Rose rather suspected it had been clawed by his daughter. "She gets in moods like this."

"I am familiar with the dangers of a petulant child when one does not have scales to protect oneself from their claws," Rose assured him. "Why don't I carry Virgil, and you pull the wagon? Your daughter can use it for now."

"Sorry," Mr. Miller apologized again, reaching out and taking the handle from her. "I'd refuse, but . . ."

"But sometimes one must choose one's battles," Rose said. "I understand. I even concur, in this instance."

Mr. Miller started walking again, and Rose continued at his pace. They were moving more briskly now that he was the one pulling the heavy wagon, rather than her.

Chapter 6: Vindicated

Cucumber let out an exultant monologue about how she had gotten the box that moved and now it was hers and now it would be hers forever.

"No, it will *not!*" Mr. Miller snapped.

The crowd tittered.

Rose waited for her son to protest, but Virgil was blithely ignoring the other dragon and all the commentary she was making about how his wagon was now her own possession. He seemed totally absorbed with shredding a crumbling brown leaf that must have blown up to him.

"You can use it for now," Mr. Miller growled, "but you cannot keep it. It belongs to the other dragon."

No, there was no other dragon. It was all Cucumber's.

"He's RIGHT THERE!" Mr. Miller shouted, pointing at Virgil in Rose's arms.

Cucumber was ignoring what her father was pointing at.

Several people near the front of the crowd doubled over and howled.

"Cucumber," her father said through clenched teeth, "you cannot pretend another person doesn't exist just because you find them inconvenient."

Cucumber didn't know what her father was talking about. Cucumber was ignoring the memories her father wanted her to look at. Yes, Cucumber was ignoring them.

She poked her claws into the side of the wagon. There was a piece she could shred off here! Look, it shredded into lots of little bitty slivers! She could shred more of it!

"If you do that again, you're getting out of the wagon," Rose informed her.

The little girl dragon immediately went still. The mean lady meant it. The mean lady thought the moving box was all hers. It wasn't hers. It was Cucumber's.

"It's not, but never mind. It can be yours for right now," Rose said, shaking her head. Virgil was still not complaining. He seemed greatly amused by his leaf, his tail twitching and his back legs mercifully still as he kept examining the brown thing.

Cucumber felt vindicated! This was her box! She had won it! It was hers! She would breathe her name into it!

"No!" Mr. Miller yelped, diving forward to grab his daughter as she reared back to breathe a tongue of flame.

The quiet son in Rose's arms looked down, seeing that the object of dispute was now vacated. Virgil wanted to be in his wagon now. Could he be in his wagon?

But Rose barely registered that. Her mind was humming with a flurry of frenzied activity.

"Breathe her *name?*" she burst out.

CHAPTER 7
Veracity

Yes, Cukie does that a lot," Mr. Miller said wearily. "She wants to breathe her name into everything. I wish she'd stop it."

"But . . . but . . ." Rose gaped at him. "Does that mean dragons have a *written language?* There's been no sign of that from Virgil's memories!"

Whether or not *Deinonychus antirrhopus* had had a written language was one of the greatest mysteries of paleontology. If the answer was now at hand, to ascertain the fact of it was of paramount urgency. It was thought that they reasonably could have had one, as there were stones scorched by dragon fire with scorchings that seemed oddly precise, yet irregular. If that was a writing system . . . if dragons had a way of writing . . .

If Cucumber could *read* it . . .

Rose felt dizzy at the implications. The knowledge that could be gained by gathering as many as possible of those stones and asking a baby dragon to interpret!

"I don't know," Mr. Miller said. "I assumed she made it up. She knows my wife and I are always writing things."

"What if she didn't?!" Rose exclaimed. "Do you understand what that could mean?!"

He shrugged. "That dragons are intelligent. We know that."

Rose gaped at him. How could he not comprehend the implications?

"It could mean that there are *written records!* Lost knowledge that wasn't just stored in an oral tradition! It might be possible to *translate it!*"

The thought of written records that predated the dawn of humanity . . . the idea of forgotten history that could be easily uncovered just by asking one who knew how to read it . . . the very concept made Rose's knees feel weak.

Yes, newly hatched infants were not ambassadors, and not intended to be emissaries of their species. They had not been sent by design, nor filled specifically with knowledge to act as time capsules for their species. Yet, despite all odds, here they were, awake and alive. And if they could be a key . . .

"Oh. Yes." Mr. Miller did not seem to grasp how milieu-shattering this revelation could be. "That would be nice."

"*Nice!*" Rose could scarcely keep her voice at reasonable levels. "Don't you understand the magnitude of how important that could be?!"

Cucumber shoved her head under her father's armpit, squirming tighter against him. She was scared of the mean lady. The mean lady was very scary.

Rose took a deep breath, trying to force herself to calm down. Her heart was racing.

Virgil butted his head against her chest. Could he go in his wagon now? He wanted to go in his wagon. He was behaving.

Her arms were shaking as she moved to put him where he wanted to be. Her mind was whirling. If dragons had a written language, why did Virgil not know about it? Why did none of his memories from his mother contain her breathing fire upon a rock to write something? She had been a studious academic in nature, just like Rose. Surely she would have recorded things in much the same way. So why was there no indication that she had done so?

Of course, there was the possibility that she was simply misunderstanding.

"C-Cucumber," Rose stammered, stumbling over the word. "Can you write your name so that I can see what it looks like?"

"I'm not sure that's the best idea," Mr. Miller said.

Cucumber would breathe her name! Cucumber wanted to breathe her name!

"On what?" Mr. Miller demanded. "You're not breathing it on the wagon."

Cucumber's father was showing memories of something that didn't exist.

"You were claiming ownership of it *one minute ago!*"

Cucumber didn't know what he was talking about. There was a green male in that moving box now, so it didn't exist.

"AHA!"

The crowd guffawed.

Maybe those nosy intruders could make themselves useful. Rose spun around to face them.

"Do you see a rock?" she demanded. "Something large that she could breathe her name on?"

"Here's one!" somebody called from the back.

The crowd moved to let a teenage boy jostle his way through. In his hand he held a loose brick.

It was probably meant to belong to some sidewalk somewhere, but never mind that. This was too important to worry about where it had come from.

"Breathe fire on this," Rose said, drawing next to Mr. Miller and his daughter.

Cucumber reared back her head.

"Your hand!" Mr. Miller exclaimed.

Rose scarcely dropped the brick in time to escape the blast of fire that came from the dragon's mouth. Sweat beaded on the back of her neck as she realized how close she had come to being badly injured.

"Here, Cukie. Breathe fire on the rock from the ground," Mr. Miller said, setting the girl dragon down.

Seeming obliging now, for a change, the little dragon rolled over to the brick and reared her head back.

Fire roared from her mouth, in several different colors simultaneously. Rose watched in awe. She had never seen Virgil do such a thing.

Then the little girl dragon rolled back over to her father and informed him that she wanted up. Up. Up. Up now.

He picked her up. She amused herself by flicking her claw upwards and seizing his hat.

Rose stared at the rock, not daring to touch it because it was doubtless still hot. There was a symbol on there of two wiggly lines, one crisscrossing the other. It did not look like a C, nor like an oblong-shaped fruit.

"What does this mean, Cucumber?" she asked, pointing to it, her heart pounding so loudly that could hear the roar in her ears. "What does this symbol mean?"

The lady was so stupid. It was Cucumber's name.

"Yes, but *how* is it your name?" Rose demanded. "Is it the fruit you were named after? Some sort of English writing, like your parents?"

Stupid! The female dragon seemed downright scornful. Cucumber's name was Cucumber's name! Cucumber's parents had given her that name, and it was Cucumber's name!

"See?" Mr. Miller said. "That's all she ever says about it."

"*Which* parents?" Rose pursued. "Was it your human parents or your dragon parents?"

Cucumber's *parent* parents! Cucumber was getting really angry!

"*Which* parents are your parent parents?"

The parents that were Cucumber's parents!

"Which ones?"

The parents that were *parents!*

"Which ones taught you to write?"

Cucumber exploded with fury. She would show her! She would show this mean lady!

Memory roared over Rose, a cascade of irresistibility, overlaid with a torrent of frustration and fury that she was fairly sure hadn't been present originally.

Chapter 7: Veracity

She was swimming around in her liquid, comfortably. Her parents moved close, so she could feel their presence.

She was greeting her parents. They were greeting her back.

Her father showed her a picture. This was her name. She would use it to mark things hers after she hatched. They had chosen it just for her. Could she show it to them back?

She showed it to them wrong, the picture.

No, no. She must get it exactly right. This was important, because her brother's name was similar. When it was time to breathe fire, she would do it this way, and that way . . .

The memory started to fade. Rose came back to herself gradually, so stunned by the memory that at first she could not remember that she had human arms and no tail that she could swish behind her while swimming through the egg.

Rose breathed in raggedly. Her arms were shaking.

That was a true memory. I cannot doubt its veracity.

As if to confirm this, Cucumber's father's eyes were wide, and he was pulling a notebook and pen from his pocket.

Then the symbol she burns isn't the name of a fruit. It's the name her birth parents originally gave her. Perhaps all of their names were visual, rather than auditory.

But how . . . how . . . how had Virgil's memories never given her any hint of this? His mother had been highly educated. So if there had been writing, surely she of all people . . .

Virgil rolled around in the wagon and poked his head up over the side. The female dragon who he wasn't thinking about and who also didn't exist had weird memories. She was making them up. Dragon parents didn't have names. Nobody had names except for human parents and their babies and also nobody could breathe fire that way. That was silly.

Rose turned around and stared at her son with an open mouth. *What . . . ?*

How could his memories contradict hers so thoroughly?

CHAPTER 8
Variance

Her first thought was, *Maybe they come from different cultures.* But no, that didn't make sense. The two had been found in the same cave, in the same area.

Her second thought was, *Maybe they come from different classes.* But that didn't make sense either. Virgil's mother, at least, had been educated.

So how could their memories of dragon society have such an irreconcilable variance? She sensed her son's sincerity, and she did not doubt the other dragon's veracity either. But how?

Why would one family have abilities that another did not, names when another did not, perhaps even a written language when another did not?

Unless . . .

Rose felt a little dizzy.

She, of all people, should have grasped the implications of this right away. Their two families had not been separated by distance. They had been separated by time.

Deinonychus antirrhopus had lived on Earth for millions of years. Over a span of millions of years, a species could grow and change. A culture certainly would.

Her son had come from a earlier time than Mr. Miller's daughter.

In fact . . . her son was evidently a significantly less evolved *Deinonychus* than Mr. Miller's daughter, because she had an ability to control her fire-breathing that he did not.

How much? How much time had separated the two?

Rose's mind flew to Violet. Violet, who remembered the extinction event. The child who lived in the zoo might be the most evolved *Deinonychus* now alive today. Could she control her fire? Had she had a name?

It was almost impossible to be sure. Rose wanted to weep with frustration. Violet's memories of her life before the zoo were so corrupted by this point that they were worthless for anything but the entertainment of the masses.

Had anyone written down the earliest memories the little blue dragon had shared? She profoundly hoped that somebody had been wiser than her.

There will be other dragons, Rose reminded herself, but it was no consolation. The loss of one unique treasure trove of history could not be ameliorated by the discovery of another.

Why had she never realized the magnitude of importance of that which was casually degrading? Why, why, why, why, why?!

All the same . . .

Rose slowed her breathing, forcing herself to calm down. All the same, she could be very grateful that she had met these two today.

Cucumber's father was scribbling hastily in his notebook, evidently desperate to capture every detail before they faded from his recollection.

Seeming to find this dull and unremarkable, the green baby girl at his feet was playing with a brown leaf, sucking it in against her mouth and then blowing it out again. At one point, a small spark escaped her nostrils, but it mercifully did not land on the leaf.

The wagon lurched as Virgil dove for the side. That was Virgil's game! The-dragon-that-didn't-exist couldn't play Virgil's game! Virgil wanted to play with that, too!

The crowd roared with laughter at her son's subsequent attempt to fling himself over the side of the wagon, his horrified yowl as he realized that if he landed below he would land on the green girl, and then his vehement complaining about how dragons who didn't exist shouldn't be playing with his leaves and toys and wagons. It wasn't fair!

Cucumber kept on playing with one leaf and then another, seemingly oblivious to the whole tantrum.

At last, Mr. Miller let out a long sigh as he completed his task and replaced the notebook in his pocket.

"That was a new memory," he said.

"I gathered," Rose nodded.

Mr. Miller's forehead creased with hurt as he stared down at his daughter, who pounced at a wind-blown leaf with claws extended. "She's never even given us the slightest *hint* of that memory before. Why wouldn't she tell us?"

"Maybe she didn't remember it until now," Rose said. "It might have been been one of her earliest memories. It might have been one that was already fuzzy by the time she started to hibernate. Sometimes . . ."

She hesitated, because she could not think of a way to phrase this that didn't make her look bad.

"Sometimes," she said at last, "when I have had . . . ah . . . disagreements with my younger sisters, an argument has brought certain details back into sharp clarity that had been previously forgotten, such as who had stolen whom's best winter stockings six months previously."

She did not add that the culprit in that case had been her.

Mr. Miller looked intrigued. "You mean, becoming upset prodded her into remembering something old she had almost forgotten?"

"Most likely," Rose said. She added wryly, "Not that that would be a reasonable approach to apply deliberately. Unless, of course, it could be employed by someone who knew how to do it in such a way that would not inappropriately upset the subject of study . . ."

Chapter 8: Variance

The idea was intriguing! *Could* the strategy be used in some appropriate way? Rose's eyes brightened as she considered the possibilities.

The man laughed out loud. "You're a strange woman, Mrs. Wainscott!"

Rose stared at him, startled. Chagrin flooded her, and she lowered her face. "Am I?"

"Oh, I don't mean that in any bad way," Mr. Miller said hastily. "I'm sure you're a great mother."

"Am I?" Rose said quietly. That was not something she felt sure about at all.

"Ah . . ." Mr. Miller bit his lower lip. He suddenly seemed to realize that he had wandered into a dangerous subject. His eyes flicked back and forth, perhaps hoping for a conversational aid from the crowd.

But the crowd was of no help to him. There were howls of deafening laughter as Cucumber blew a leaf up into the air, it landed on Virgil's face, and the baby boy let out a furious tirade about how the wind had blown the leaf up into his face, and the wind had stolen his wagon, and the wind was really mean, and — oh, hey, now he had a leaf!

"I think anyone can be a good parent," Mr. Miller said quickly. "You just have to find a way to use your own strengths for your children's benefit."

Rose gave him a look of polite disbelief. She did not think her own strengths translated at all to being a good parent. That was why she felt so inadequate at it.

"It's true! I'll give you an example," the man said, stumbling over his words in his haste to correct his accidental faux pas. "You're good at . . . uh . . ."

"Paleontology," Rose said dryly. She failed to see how that had any relevance to nurturing living beings.

"There you go!" the man said with relief. "You know all about dragons! That has to translate to being very good at taking care of him, right?"

"I am not a nurse," Rose said, with some annoyance.

"I didn't say you *were*. But . . . correct me if I'm wrong, but isn't that the field with people who dig up fossils? Like the ones who found Cukie's egg?"

"Yes," Rose said.

"I've been told that takes a lot of patience. And a lot of being careful about every tiny detail. Is that the case?"

"Yes. It is a highly methodical discipline."

"Well, don't you think that patience and being very careful are strengths that can be useful in parenting?"

Rose stared at him.

And stared at him.

She had never been particularly patient with Virgil. And she had never thought her detail-oriented mindset to be an advantage in dealing with him, because it led to such frustration when she could not control the actions of a living being, and that being's actions all too often resulted in a chaos she had to clean.

She had been measuring herself by the standards that she believed all mothers had to measure up to, and she had been failing abominably. But perhaps there was more than one adequate template.

Had she . . . had she perhaps . . . taken the wrong approach with Virgil from the very beginning?

CHAPTER 9
Virgil

She had made herself a promise all those months ago. A promise to never look upon Virgil as a subject of study. A promise to separate him from her love of fossils and remnants of antiquity, and to see him only as a child who needed loving.

Had she been wrong?

Had she miscalculated?

Virgil's birth mother, the dragon whom Rose so closely resembled, had not particularly wanted to have a child. She'd accepted the surprise grudgingly, and had continued to be rather grumpy at the egg's repeated interruptions. She had not exactly been Rose's idea of an ideal parent.

And yet, she was the mother Virgil had wanted.

That was why Virgil had chosen Rose.

For the exact same reasons that she felt so inadequate.

Rose drew in a deep, shaky breath. If Virgil had wanted her for that very mindset . . . *should* she be treating him in a manner that was affectionless and calculating?

She felt like she was dangling over a precipice. It was like the universe held its breath, waiting for her to decide.

Was it better to give Virgil what he had wanted?

Or was that different from what he *needed*?

Rose let out a long, deep sigh.

It would be so much easier to give up on trying to nurture the boy . . . and she had a fantastic excuse to do so. But she could not make herself believe that surrendering to what was easiest for her would be to his benefit.

Infants were not always wise. Even if he had chosen her for her weaknesses, that didn't mean she ought to wallow in them.

Still . . . there might be a grain of truth in the man's words. In her determination to shield Virgil from her weaknesses, perhaps she had been withholding her strengths from him, too.

Rose laughed wryly, overcome with realization.

On the day they'd first met, Virgil had shown her memories of rejecting many parents. Many, many, many, many parents. Because they were not exactly like the ones he remembered, and he wouldn't take new parents unless they were exactly like his old ones. And why had he never found an exact equivalent of his birth mother until Rose?

Because someone like the two of them would not have gone looking for a child to adopt in the first place.

Rose shook her head, still laughing at the irony of her son's absurdity. No wonder he was so old, compared to Cucumber. Perhaps he was one of the oldest *Deinonychus antirrhopus* eggs that would hatch. He had been waiting for a very long time to find a mother who didn't want him. Because only a mother who didn't want him could possibly do.

She had to laugh, because otherwise she would start to cry, and if she started to cry, she wouldn't stop. Why had Virgil put her in this impossible situation? Choosing her precisely because she was the wrong person?

". . . Mrs. Wainscott?" Mr. Miller asked, looking concerned.

Rose quickly shook herself, realizing she was surrounded by people. Fortunately, the crowd seemed thoroughly absorbed in watching and laughing at the antics of the babies, and the babies were so absorbed in goofing off to entertain the eager crowd that they were paying no attention to their parents. She had not expected to be grateful for the raucous mob, but . . .

Chapter 9: Virgil

Silently, Rose observed the infants that the crowd found so amusing.

Virgil was now whacking his tail at leaves that "the wind" blew up at him, chattering eagerly about how whacking his tail at leaves was fun. Cucumber, meanwhile, was blowing leaves up at the wagon, commenting at how funny it was that "the wind" kept sending them flying in strange directions.

It seemed the two of them had found a way to play together after all, still without acknowledging the other's existence.

A slight smile curled on her lips. Her son was certainly strange, and the boy could be entertaining.

And with that faint amusement came a sense of peace that surprised her. It was not what she would have expected at this moment, yet it was there.

Perhaps . . .

Perhaps it didn't matter that she was so unqualified to be the best sort of parent. Any mother Virgil would have chosen would have been exactly like her.

Perhaps it didn't matter that she had messed up so many things.

Perhaps the only thing that mattered was that he had chosen *her*, and she could choose to get better.

"Mrs. Wainscott?" Mr. Miller ventured again.

Rose tried to ignore the stab of irritation at his intrusion into her thoughts. He had helped her realize several things today, after all.

She drew in a deep breath. "I am fine, Mr. Miller. It was simply . . . something I had not considered. Thank you for the insight. I will think upon it further."

"Oh, good." He looked relieved.

The rest of the visit with Cucumber and her father remained uneventful, with Mr. Miller carefully avoiding any subjects that resembled the one that had made her emotional, and Rose succeeding in extracting no new memories from either dragon, despite her repeated and fruitless attempts to interest them in being interviewed instead of playing with "the wind."

Eventually, after an hour had passed without their moving any farther down the sidewalk, Mr. Miller remarked on the time and they made their farewells, to the groaning disappointment of the crowd around them. It was not comprised of all of the same people who had been there at the beginning, but it had swelled to more than five times the original size, nonetheless.

As she turned towards the apartment to go back home, shivering as a brisk breeze picked up, Virgil complained vehemently from in his wagon. He was cold and he wanted to play more with the wind and now the wind was all gone.

Rose snorted, brushing the strands of hair out of her mouth that a puff of chill air had blown in there.

Also he was hungry. Virgil was hungry! Virgil wanted to eat chicken, chicken, chicken, all by itself!

"For crying out loud, Virgil," she said in exasperation, wanting to kick herself for forgetting that playing out in the cold would make him hungrier than playing indoors or staying under a warm blanket. "You can wait till dinner."

Virgil wanted chickennnnnnnnn!

"You weren't so hungry while you were playing with that green girl dragon," Rose said acerbically.

Virgil didn't know what his mother was talking about. Green girl dragons didn't exist. He had been playing with the wind.

"You were playing with a green girl dragon, and you know it."

No! Virgil had not been! Virgil's mother was being mean!

"Virgil's mother does not approve of self-deception," Rose retorted, glancing back at the wagon as she walked briskly forward. "Virgil's mother thinks that he can play with whoever he wants, but it's ridiculous to pretend he didn't."

Virgil had been playing with THE WIND!

"Honestly!" Rose said, shaking her head at the memory of the two dragons' fear of one another. Interesting as it had been at first, the situation had quickly devolved into sheer absurdity. "Can you imagine what would happen if humans acted that way?"

Humans *did* act that way!

"No, we do not."

Yes, they did!

"No, we don't."

Yes, they did! Virgil's mother acted that way about Ophelia's parents!

Rose froze.

Anyway, Virgil hadn't been playing with a green girl dragon. He had been playing with the wind.

Rose closed her eyes and touched her forehead with her free hand. She stood still, holding the wagon handle with her other. *It isn't just their color. It's also that they're so polite that if I made some terrible faux pas, they wouldn't tell me. I don't know the rules of propriety, and if I made mistakes . . .*

And THE WIND was fun, and THE WIND had blown the leaves around, and Virgil had been playing with THE WIND . . .

"All right, Virgil!" Rose shouted, spinning around to glare at her son. "I get the message! I'll ask for the Lawrences' phone number when we get home, and I'll call them! Are you happy?"

Virgil stared up at her from the wagon. No, he wasn't happy. He was hungry. Playing with the wind had made him hungry. Could he have chicken, chicken, chicken, all by itself? Also, he hadn't been playing with a green girl dragon. Green girl dragons didn't exist.

CHAPTER 10
Vitamins

When Henry walked in the door, he stopped abruptly and held his nose.

"What is that smell?!" he cried.

"Liver," Rose said, coming out of the kitchen. Her hands were still covered in red juice from chopping up chicken livers. She hadn't yet washed them.

"Why are you cooking liver?! I hate liver!"

"It's for Virgil," Rose said. "Advice from the Lawrences. Mrs. Lawrence said that organ meat is usually cheaper, and it tends to contain more vitamins."

"There's a reason why it's cheaper! It's disgusting!"

"You don't have to eat it," Rose said. "But it's nutritious for him, and it might be the solution to our budgetary problems."

Henry held his nose. "Could you at least not *cook* it?"

Virgil rolled out of the kitchen and into the living room, a blackened lump dangling from one side of his mouth.

Rose began, "I didn't —"

Hello! Virgil was saying hello to his father! He had made up a fun game of singe-the-prey because somebody — that was, somebody-that-didn't-exist — had shown him a memory of her parents doing it! Prey tasted much better when he breathed fire on it! He was going to do this all the time from now on!

Chapter 10: Vitamins

"We've given you cooked meat before, Virgil," Rose said.

But *this* food tasted *much* better when it was black all over, and Virgil could do it all by himself, and that was much more fun! Yummy, yummy, yummy, yummy!

Henry looked woebegone. "So I get to smell charcoal, as well as liver, every day from now on?"

"How about I take him outside to eat the rest of his meal?" Rose asked, picking up their son with her messy hands. "He can eat outside whenever he's hungry."

"No . . ." Henry sighed heavily, releasing the death grip on his nose. "I've gotten used to the smell of his diapers. I can get used to this."

Rose quirked a smile. "You're a brave man."

"You'd better believe it," Henry said, shaking his head. He walked over and reached out for the happy baby, who eagerly lunged into his arms. "Have you been good for your mother's birthday?"

Rose started. She had nearly forgotten that was today.

Yes! Virgil had been very good! He had gotten to try new food that he liked way better, and his mother hadn't made him eat eggs, and he'd played with the wind, and there hadn't been a dragon that didn't exist —

"Say what?" Henry asked, looking perplexed.

Virgil's tail swung back and forth as he explained that they had gone to the zoo to play with a dragon, only it wasn't a zoo and it wasn't a dragon, it was GREEN GREEN GREEN, but then it had been fine, and there was no such thing as a girl, and anyway it was the wind he had been playing with . . .

Henry looked at his wife in absolute bafflement.

Rose bit back a laugh. "It's a long and ridiculous story."

Two days later, on the morning of Valentine's Day, they walked to Rose's parents' house and delivered Virgil to spend the day there.

"Hello, Rose! Hello, Henry!" Rose's mother said, opening the front door to welcome them in. "Hello, Virgil!"

Their son poked his head out of the top of Henry's coat. He had been nestled in there for warmth the whole trip.

Hello! Virgil was saying hello to his grandmother!

"Would you like to help us make Valentines, Virgil?" Rose's mother asked, taking the little dragon from Henry.

Virgil didn't know what Valentines were.

"They're usually heart-shaped —" Henry began.

Virgil LIKED hearts! Virgil's mother had bought him hearts! Hearts were really yummy! Yum yum yum yum!

"Noooot quite the same," Henry said.

Rose wandered to the living room table, where she saw a scattering of paper and printed cards. As Sara leaned over Louise's shoulder to watch what she was writing, a burst of mischievous giggles broke forth from both of them.

"What exactly are you doing?" Rose asked suspiciously.

"Nothing," her two younger sisters chorused.

Given that both of them were in high school, she judged them to have just enough experience to get into a lot of trouble, and not nearly enough good sense to stay out of it. Rose stalked over and plucked the printed card from Louise's hands.

"Hey!" Louise complained.

Rose scanned the card. It seemed like typical, sentimental fare. She couldn't see any especial reason for her sisters' high amusement. "Is Harrison the name of a boy in your school?"

Louise giggled. "Nooooo."

"Is he someone at church?"

Sara snickered. "Nooooo."

"Who is it, then?"

The two girls guffawed.

Rose dropped the card on the table. "Not Harrison Jones!"

Her sisters howled with laughter.

Harrison Jones was the father of Violet, the dragon who lived in the zoo. He was a rough man, single, and fond of drink. Despite the fact that alcohol was illegal.

Chapter 10: Vitamins

"You find him attractive?" Rose asked in mystification.

"No!" Louise giggled. "But if he *thinks* I do, maybe he'll marry me and then Violet can be my pet dragon!"

"LOUISE!" Rose shouted. "That is appalling on so many levels, I can't even count!"

Her sisters laughed so hard that they struggled to breathe.

"Try *not* to be preposterously rude to Mr. Jones," Rose scolded. "He has enough troubles in his life already."

That just made them laugh harder.

"Shall we go now?" Henry asked, following Rose into the living room.

"Certainly," she said, giving her sisters one last disapproving glare as she returned to the entrance with her husband. They were still tittering as she gave her mother a hug and promised to come back by dinnertime.

She and Henry exited the building, crunching out into the relative quiet of the sidewalk, flakes slowly drifting around them and filling in the grey churning in the streets by car tires and horse hooves.

"Where's the big Valentine surprise?" Henry asked eagerly.

"We'll be there soon," Rose said. "Be patient."

And I hope it is a present he'll like, she added silently.

CHAPTER 11
Value

"The museum?" Henry asked as she turned to enter its doors and beckoned for Henry to follow. "What are we doing here?"

"We're here for Valentine's Day," Rose said. "Trust me."

Looking a little disappointed, Henry followed after her. The two went up floor after floor. At the top of the stairs, Henry started to head for the Hall of Saurischian Dragons, the place where they had met Virgil. But Rose stopped him.

"Not there," she said, pointing. "There."

"The Hall of Ornithischian Dragons?" he asked in confusion.

"Trust me," she said.

"We met Virgil in the Hall of Saurischian Dragons," she said. "But you were heading to the Hall of Ornithischian Dragons at the time. I used to spend equal amounts of time in both rooms. If it hadn't been for Virgil, we might very well have met on the same day while you were sketching the wings of a *Stegosaurus*. We can think of it as our place."

For a heartbeat, Henry was silent.

Rose swallowed. *Does he not like . . . ?*

Henry smiled, at last. "I can see that," he said. "Well, then, let's go into our place."

They walked into the room hand in hand.

Chapter 11: Value

Together, they admired the fossils, taking their time and discussing every detail they saw. Henry had a remarkable eye, and described interesting details of shape and theories about dragon colors that she had not thought to consider before.

"Well . . ." Henry said, looking around.

"Wait," Rose told him, holding up her hand. "There's one more thing."

"One more thing?" he asked.

"Yes," she nodded. "I'll be right back."

She hurried out of the room and walked briskly down the hallway to Mr. Teedle's office. She had told him to expect her at around this time, and he had told her he would stay either on or near his office until he saw her.

Fortunately, when she knocked on his office, her oldest friend was sitting there, filling out a form.

"Hello, Miss Pal— Mrs. Wainscott," he said, smiling. "Do you want the present?"

"Yes," she nodded.

He reached behind his desk and picked up a box of sand. It was not very large, but because of all the sand filling it, it was heavy. "Can you manage on your own?"

"I'll manage," Rose said, taking it from him. "Thank you for holding it for me."

"You're very welcome. I hope he likes it."

It was heavier than she'd expected, but she managed to carry it down the hallway back to the Hall of Ornithischian Dragons, where Henry was waiting. From the back, she could see that he had pulled his sketchbook out of his pocket and was penciling the curve of a duck-billed dragon.

Rose set down the box, wanting to wait for him to be done with the *Anatotitan*. She tried to be quiet, but it made a rather loud *thump*.

Henry turned around. "Oh! You're back!"

He put the sketchbook away.

Rose swallowed. This was the important part. This was the part she had spent all of yesterday preparing.

"I . . . I love paleontology," she said. "As a child, my fascination started from the concept of digging up buried treasure. So I thought . . . I would share that with you. Your present's in here."

"In the sand?"

"Yes."

"I'm supposed to dig in the sand?"

"There's a brush in here somewhere," Rose said hastily. She ran her hands through the sand until she found it, and then pushed the sand back over the top.

Henry looked bemused. He took the brush from her and knelt down next to the box. Then he brushed the sand away, not nearly as carefully as he should have, but the contents were not fossils, so she wouldn't say so.

He found a drawstring cloth bag and carefully shook the sand off of it. Then he opened it. Inside was a notebook.

Looking puzzled, Henry opened the notebook to reveal pages of Rose's tiny, tidy handwriting. Grains of sand rolled down and fell into the box.

"I recently realized that we should be recording Virgil's memories," Rose said, as he flipped silently through the pages. "Because that will be of value. But then I realized that there's something even more important, and that's our memories of each other. So . . . . this is our story from the past year. Every detail I remember. Which is to say, not everything, but a lot. I'm fairly certain I got all the dates correct, for instance. I have a better memory for details than most. I thought maybe I should use the things I'm good at to benefit you."

Henry said nothing. He was just flipping through pages.

Rose felt a lump in her throat. Did he not like it? She was terribly worried. She hadn't spent much money on this. Suppose Henry thought she was being cheap?

Henry put his hand over an blank square of space she had left in a corner. "There are empty spots," he said.

"I thought you might want to draw pictures there."

Henry looked up. There were tears in his eyes.

"Thank you," he said. "It's a great Valentine's Day present."

Chapter 11: Value

Rose let out a deep breath. "Oh, good! I wasn't sure!"

Henry laughed.

"If you want to, we could make this a tradition," Rose said. "Every Valentine's Day, we come here and we share the past year's memories we've made together. Not our memories of Virgil, just . . . us."

"I'd like that," Henry said, holding the notebook tightly across his chest. "I'd like that a lot."

"We could do the same thing for Virgil's birthday, too," Rose went on quickly. "I could write things down, and you could draw the way things look in his memories —"

"Shhh." Henry put his finger on Rose's lips. "No Virgil right now. Just . . . us."

www.ingramcontent.com/pod-product-compliance
Lightning Source LLC
Chambersburg PA
CBHW022121050726

47591CB00002B/888